GREATEST ANIMAL STORIES

Chosen By

MICHAEL MORPURGO

This book belongs to:

_____

For Jonathan and his family, with our thanks.

First edition for the United States and Canada published in 2017
by Barron's Educational Series, Inc.
Selection and arrangement copyright © Michael Morpurgo 2016

Greatest Animal Stories was originally published in English
in 2016. This edition is published by arrangement with
Oxford University Press.
All rights reserved.

All inquiries should be addressed to:
Barron's Educational Series, Inc.
250 Wireless Boulevard
Hauppauge, NY 11788
www.barronseduc.com

ISBN: 978-1-4380-5003-4
Library of Congress Control Number: 2017931440

Date of Manufacture: June 2017
Manufactured by: Leo Paper Products, Heshan, China

Printed in China
9 8 7 6 5 4 3 2 1

GREATEST ANIMAL STORIES

Chosen By

MICHAEL MORPURGO

BARRON'S

Introduction

For so many children—and I know this because I was a child too, once—our first contact with animals is through stories and pictures. I knew my first elephant, my first bear, and my first toad from legends, myths, and folk tales. I heard the story of the *Ugly Duckling* before I had ever watched the magic of a cygnet transforming into a swan and listened to *Peter and the Wolf* before I had seen a prowling, predatory wolf in the flesh. Through fables such as Aesop's, fairy tales such as *Puss in Boots*, and ancient stories such as *Noah's Ark*, I met a whole world of amazing animals. These stories led me to my love of the countryside and my fascination not just with animals, but our relationship to them—how close we can feel to them, how they can comfort us and console us, amuse us and entertain us, how we respect and love them, but also how often we abuse their trust, how we exploit and destroy them.

I grew up for much of my childhood on the coast of Essex, walking the sea wall, leaning into the wild wind, looking out over the great brown soupy North Sea, with the gulls crying and the oystercatchers piping. There were hares and foxes and deer to see in the fields, along with cows and sheep, larks and herons, and swallows and kestrels. The place was alive with the creatures I had discovered in stories. And later, as a teacher, I thought every child should know nature this closely and might come to love it as I had. So, with my wife Clare, we began Farms for City Children, forty years ago now, a charity that still enables thousands of city and town children to experience the world of nature, the countryside and farming, first hand.

Not surprising then that, as any writer does, I turned to the world of what I knew and cared about—animals and nature and children—to fill my stories. In this book you will find some of the stories that inspired me, stories I grew up with and loved when I was young—many of my favorite tales, told wonderfully well by some of the best writers we have today. They are great stories from great writers, stories that have stood the test of time, many told to children for hundreds of years. Enjoy them, and then maybe dream up your own animal stories and poems. That's how *Mog* began or the *Gruffalo*, or *Paddington* or *Peter and the Wolf*, any of the stories you love. Someone like you, like me, just sat down and wrote their dreamed up story, told it onto the page or screen so that we could all enjoy it.

Michael Morpurgo

Contents

Have you ever seen a dog with a bone? And if you did see one, would you ever try to take the bone away? I wouldn't if I were you. And I don't think Aesop would, either. Aesop may have written this fable over 2,500 years ago, but his stories, and the lessons in them, are timeless. Dogs will always love bones, and dogs (and people) will always be tempted by what they don't have. But remember, if you're too greedy, then you may risk what you already have . . .

The Dog and His Reflection

Retold by Joanna Nadin

Illustrated by Irina Troitskaya

Once upon a time there was a greedy dog. He didn't think his own food was enough, so he stole from his friends when they weren't looking.

"How rude," moaned Cat, whose milk had disappeared for the third time that week.

"It's not fair," groaned Goat, whose scraps had vanished into thin air, or rather, into Dog.

But Cow was wise. She told them, "Be patient. Dog
will get his comeuppance one day soon."

This went on for months and months. Dog stole food,
and Cat and Goat moaned and groaned.

But Cow always said the same thing: "Be patient. Dog will get his comeuppance one day soon."

One day, Dog went for a long walk to town and spotted a bone in the tailor's backyard. It was meant for the tailor's Wolfhound, but Dog wanted it for himself.

So, when Wolfhound was busy with a ball and the tailor was busy with his mending, Dog snuck through the gate and snapped up the bone. Then he trotted off in the direction of home, with his treasure firmly between his teeth.

Along the way was a ford, which is a small river that runs right across a road.

As he was crossing the ford, Dog looked down and was surprised to see another dog that looked just like him.

What's more, this dog had a bone between his teeth, too. But Dog thought this other bone looked far nicer than his, and greed got the better of him.

"It's even bigger and more juicy," said Dog to himself. "I must have it!"

But when he opened his mouth to take the bone, his own bone fell from his jaws. It floated away down the river.

"I don't care," said greedy Dog. "Because now I have the bigger, juicier bone!"

But when he tried to snap up the bigger, juicier bone, he got a shock! That one was sailing down the river, too. And in the end, Dog was forced to slink home, his stomach empty and his tail between his legs.

"Not thirsty?" asked Cat, when Dog didn't try to take her milk.

"Not hungry?" asked Goat, when Dog didn't try to steal his scraps.

"No," said Dog. "I'm full already."

But Dog wasn't full. He was feeling foolish because he had lost his perfectly good bone trying to snap up a better one.

Only Cow was wise and guessed the truth.
She also guessed that Dog had learned
his lesson, and he would never be greedy again.
And she was right.

MORAL

If you're greedy, you might lose out
on the good things you already have.

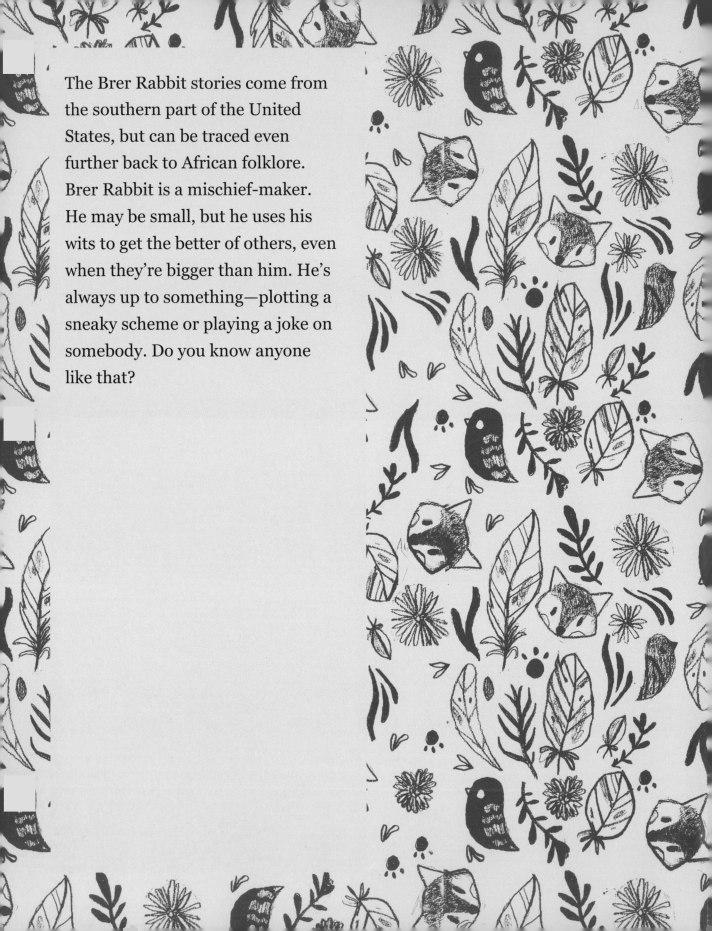

The Brer Rabbit stories come from the southern part of the United States, but can be traced even further back to African folklore. Brer Rabbit is a mischief-maker. He may be small, but he uses his wits to get the better of others, even when they're bigger than him. He's always up to something—plotting a sneaky scheme or playing a joke on somebody. Do you know anyone like that?

Brer Rabbit and the Well

Retold by Tony Bradman

Illustrated by Steve Horrocks

It was a beautiful day and the sun was shining down on Brer Rabbit as he hopped through the fields. Now usually he would be looking for someone to play a trick on. But he felt very hot, so he was looking for something cool to drink instead.

At last, he came to an old well. You had to lower the bucket and fill it with water, then haul it back up again to drink. Brer Rabbit started to do that . . . but then he stopped.

How lovely it would be to get right into the water, he thought.

So he jumped on a bucket and **whizzed** down.
Another bucket passed him on the way, shooting
upward, but he took no notice. He hit the water with
a great **splash**, and swam and drank, and drank and
swam until he felt much cooler.

Then a nasty thought occurred to him. He realized
he couldn't haul himself out of the well—and his
bucket wouldn't go up until someone lowered the
other one.

"Oh no!" he said. "I could be trapped down here for days. Help! Help!"

"You must be joking, Brer Rabbit," said a mocking voice far above him.

Brer Rabbit looked up and saw that it was Brer Fox.

"I've been watching you," Brer Fox continued, "and I know you can't get out. But you can stay there forever as far as I'm concerned!"

Things were going from bad to worse for Brer Rabbit.
He'd played a lot of tricks on Brer Fox, so
he knew he'd get no help from him.
But then Brer Rabbit had an idea.
Brer Fox was very greedy—he
simply couldn't resist the offer
of food.

"Oh well," he said. "I suppose
I'll just have to eat all these
fish myself."

"Fish?" said Brer Fox. "Er . . .
what are they like? Are they
very tasty?"

"You'd better come down and find out for yourself," said Brer Rabbit. "All you have to do is jump in that bucket and you'll soon be having a fishy feast!"

"Fantastic!" said Brer Fox.

He jumped on the bucket at the top of the well and **whizzed** down. Brer Rabbit had already made sure he was sitting on the other bucket, so he **whizzed** up. The two of them passed each other halfway.

Brer Fox hit the water with a big **splash** and jumped off the bucket.

"Hey, hang on a minute," he yelled.
"I don't see any fish down here . . ."

"Ah, I might have been fibbing
about that," said Brer Rabbit. "Bye!"

Then he hopped away with a huge
smile on his face.

27

Do you ever feel as if you don't fit in? It can be hard when that happens, but this fairy tale, written in Denmark by Hans Christian Andersen, teaches us not to hide who we really are. The strength we need to be ourselves, and to have others accept us, comes from within.

The Ugly Duckling

Retold by Geraldine McCaughrean

Illustrated by Alex Wilson
and David Pavon

At last! *Tap-tap crackle-crackle peep-peep!* One by one, Mrs. Duck's eggs broke open, and out struggled her little chicks. Golden and fluffy and adorable, they peeped their way, like a little yellow traffic jam, toward the riverbank.

But Mrs. Duck glanced back and saw that one egg was left, unhatched—an egg much bigger than the rest. "Wait a moment, children," she said.

Her neighbor took a look. "That's not a duck egg. Wrong color. That there's a turkey egg," she said.

What to do? Leave it to get cold? Or sit on it a little longer, just to be sure?

Next day, the big egg crackled, and two great, big feet stuck out.

"It does have very big feet," Mrs. Duck said to her neighbor.

"Told you. Turkey. I said, didn't I? Didn't I say? Nothing to do with you."

But Mrs. Duck had stood and sat guard over the egg for so long that she felt a kind of fondness for the hulking, scruffy object that spilled out of it.

"Put that in the river and it'll drown like a brick," said her neighbor. "That's a turkey, is that."

But it did not sink. The ugly
duckling—oh, and it had a face
only its mother could love—
took to swimming like . . . well,
like a duck to water. Dipping
his head below the water,
he tasted green weed and it
tasted almost like happiness.
In fact, he swam even
better than the other little
ducklings.

Oh, those pretty, fluffy,
delightful, *spiteful* little
ducklings!

"Ugly—blurch."

"Why are you so ugly?"

"Too big!"

"Big feet! Big feet!"

His brothers and sisters peeped and pecked at the ugly duckling and tried to drive him away. They were afraid that their friends would laugh at them for having such a lumpy, dumpy, frumpy brother.

"It looks like a tennis ball that has been chewed by a large dog," declared the Grand Duckchess, looking down her nose. "*Must* we look at that ugly face every day? It spoils the view."

And all of this the ugly duckling heard. He heard every birdy word. Pushed and pecked and poked, he learned to keep away from the other ducks. In fact, he moved farther and farther away, till he found himself walking, waddling, stumbling, wading, and swimming away and away toward the sunset.

The sun, too, moved away
for the winter, and the fields
and marshes, the lanes and
winds grew colder. Ugly Duckling
hid himself away on the salt marshes,
where the reeds rattled like feather
quills, and the water lay ankle deep.
Falling asleep one night, he did not see
the ice creeping closer over the water,
and he woke to find he could not move.

A farmer came by and saw him, kicked
the ice and broke it like an eggshell,
hatching Ugly Duckling a second time.
The kind farmer took him home to a
warm house, where the children flung
their arms wide in welcome.

It was a terrifying sight, like scarecrows blowing in a gale, gigantic creatures who ran toward him.

Ugly Duckling ran, too, in a panic—around and around the little cottage, knocking over bowls and stools and toddlers and buckets . . . The farmer's wife shrieked, the children laughed, the door opened, and a boot kicked Ugly Duckling out into wintertime.

Feather snow was falling. In fact, Ugly Duckling looked up to see what bird had shed its feathers, and saw six swans flying overhead. The sight was so beautiful that it pierced his heart like a fish hook and drew it up into the sky. For a moment, just for a moment.

He had never seen such birds before, and though they passed over in silence, he heard a kind of singing, more beautiful than any lark.

At last, a lark sang! Ugly Duckling woke. Somehow he had waddled his weary way through winter and into warmer weather.

He would stay among the reeds, even so. He had learned: There was nothing waiting for him out in the wide world but kicks and unkindness. He was just too ugly to be seen by eyes, so he resolved to stay hidden from everyone.

Still, the river called to him. His big black feet longed to push a path through flowing water, to feel the current under him like the rush of his own bloodstream! He must swim in the river one last time! *Uh-oh.*

There, on the river, was a family of swans. Where to go?
Where to hide himself? Beauty cannot bear ugliness. So,
obviously, these lovely, regal creatures would hate and
detest him. Ugly Duckling upended himself, plunging his
head deep underwater. When he could hold his breath no
longer, he resurfaced . . . and found himself under attack!
The swans were rushing toward him, necks outstretched,
black beaks ready to slice him in pieces!

Well, let them. Ugly Duckling stretched his head up high. At least he would die bravely!

"Little brother! Princeling! Friend! Where is your flock? Where is your skein? Where have you been hiding yourself?" And their necks rubbed his, flexing, stroking, caressing him. The swans did not hate him!

From the riverbank came the sound of the farmer's children.

Uh-oh!

They began to throw things.

Cake crumbs and bread crusts and words.

"A new one, look!"

"Oh, he's the best one, look."

"Yes! Isn't he just the most beautiful swan who ever swam!"

Ugly Duckling bent his head and looked down at the sunlit water. His reflection looked back at him—a majestic swan, white as the clouds above, and plumed with happiness.

In fact, that swan was more wonderfully happy than any duck has been, in the whole quacking history of the rolling river.

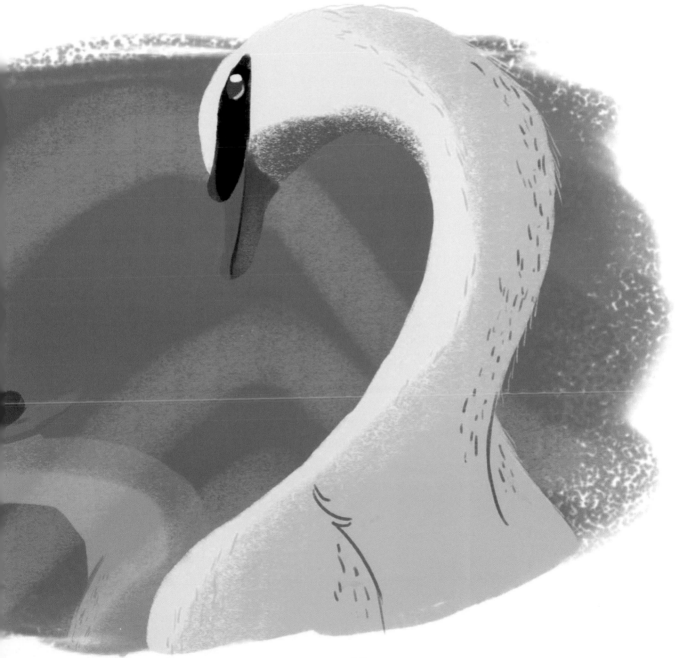

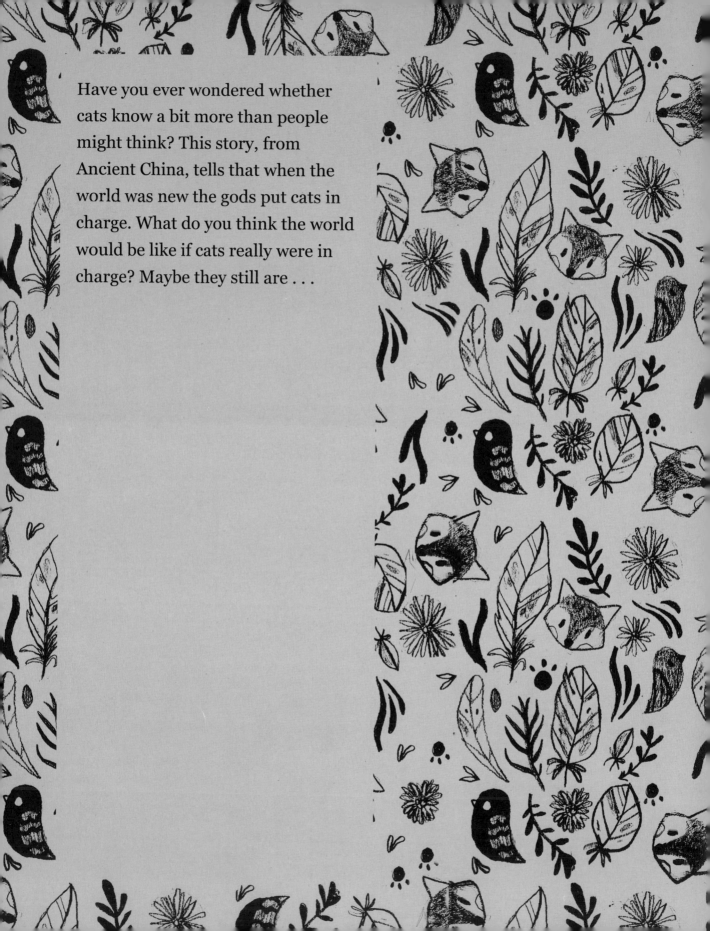

Have you ever wondered whether cats know a bit more than people might think? This story, from Ancient China, tells that when the world was new the gods put cats in charge. What do you think the world would be like if cats really were in charge? Maybe they still are . . .

When a Cat Ruled the World

Retold by Elizabeth Laird

Illustrated by Meilo So

At the very beginning of time, the world was bright and new and shiny. But the gods had a problem.

"Who's going to be in charge?" they asked each other. "Somebody needs to run the place, or things will go wrong."

At that moment, a cat walked past. He looked serious and clever. He looked as if he was thinking great thoughts. The gods looked at each other and nodded.

"That's the one," they all said. "He'll be a perfect leader."

And so the cat became the ruler of the world.

The cat was clever, but he was also very lazy. He didn't like working. He liked to lie in the sunshine. He liked to lick his paws and think about mice.

After a while, the gods decided to visit the world and see how it was going.

"How are things down here?" one of them asked the cat. "Any problems? The world is running smoothly, isn't it?"

"Well, if you must know," said the cat, "I'm not sure. I've been busy chasing butterflies."

"If you are the ruler of the world, you'll have to do more than chase butterflies!" another god said sternly. "Please try harder."

"Try harder?" yawned the cat. "Oh yes, if you like. You can rely on me."

But the cat didn't try harder. The cherry trees were in bloom. Pink and white blossoms were falling down onto the grass. The cat was having far too much fun playing with them to think about ruling the world.

A little while later, the gods came back again.

"Why are you playing around in the cherry blossoms?" they said impatiently. "There's a world to run! What about doing some work for a change?"

"Work? Running the world? Oh yes, sorry, I forgot," said the cat. "I'll stop playing and get on with it. I promise."

Off went the gods, hoping for the best. But as soon as they had gone, the cat felt rather tired.

"I'll just have a little nap," he said to himself. "I'll start ruling the world when I wake up."

But when he woke up from his nap, he wanted to wash his ears.

Then a mouse came by and he chased it for a while.

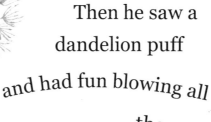

Then he saw a dandelion puff and had fun blowing all the seeds away.

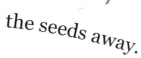

The gods came back for a third time.

"It's no good," said the cat, before they could say a word. "I can't rule the world. Work is just too boring! There are so many other things that I want to do. Couldn't you find someone else to look after everything?"

The gods frowned. They were angry. The cat had let them down.

Then the cat had an idea. "I know!" he said. "There are animals with two legs running around everywhere. They're always trying to boss the rest of us around. They poke their noses into everyone's business. Wouldn't they do?"

"Oh, you mean the people," said the gods. "Well, we could make them the rulers of the world. But if we do, we'll have to take something away from you and give it to them."

"Take anything you like!" said the cat. "I don't mind, as long as I can just please myself. Look, there's a leaf falling over there. I must go and chase it!"

And off he ran.

"You won't be able to talk anymore!" the gods shouted after him. "We'll take away your power of speech and give it to the people!"

But the cat didn't hear.
He was having too much fun
playing with the falling leaves.

From that day on, no cat ever said a word. The people began to talk instead. And, once the people started to talk, there was no stopping them!

The people worked hard looking after the world.

They liked being in charge. And the cats? The cats were happy, too. They had all the time in the world to play, and sleep, and chase after mice.

The gods still felt that the cats should help in some way. So they made the cats into walking clocks. To this very day, in the early morning, you will notice that the eyes of cats are round and dark and deep.

As the sun gets higher in the sky, their eyes change into slits.

53

In the evening, they open out into round pools of blackness again.

There's another reason why cats are still important. When you hear them purr, you are hearing the wheels that turn the world. If the cats stopped purring, the world would stop moving. There would be no day and no night, no summer and no winter.

So now you know why cats are so smug. They know they are clever and important, but they are also free. They do whatever they want, whenever they want.

If you've ever been tempted to pretend to be someone that you're not, I think the story about the wolf who disguises himself as a sheep should be enough to make you think twice. The wolf may think that his trick will get him a good dinner, but all he ends up with is a lot of trouble.

The Wolf in Sheep's Clothing

Retold by Pie Corbett

Illustrated by Ester Garcia Cortes

Once upon a time there was a sly old wolf. He was as skinny as a snake and hungry for meat.

One day, the wolf saw a flock of sheep on the hillside. There was snow on the ground and it was very cold. A shepherd was busy feeding the sheep. He called them by their names and patted their backs.

The shepherd cared for his flock, but to the wolf they were nothing more than lamb chops.

Later that day, the wolf was out hunting on the snowy hillside. He found a sheepskin under a tree. An idea popped into the wolf's head. Perhaps he could dress up as a sheep and join the flock!

What a clever disguise! The shepherd would never guess. The wolf could eat the sheep one by one without anyone knowing.

The wolf felt his belly rumble!

In the evening, when the sun was setting, the wolf dressed himself in the sheepskin. The sheep were tired and cold. A few of them bleated when they saw him, but all they wanted was the warmth of their pen.

The wolf snuggled down with the sheep. There were more Sunday dinners here than in his wildest dreams . . .

But his plan was not as clever as he had hoped.
The shepherd wanted some meat
for his dinner.

He went down to the pen
and chose the thinnest-
looking sheep.

63

He killed it and took it home for his wife to roast.
But they had quite a shock, for it was not a sheep that
he had killed. It was the wolf!

The shepherd thanked his lucky stars that he had
killed the wolf and saved the rest of the flock.

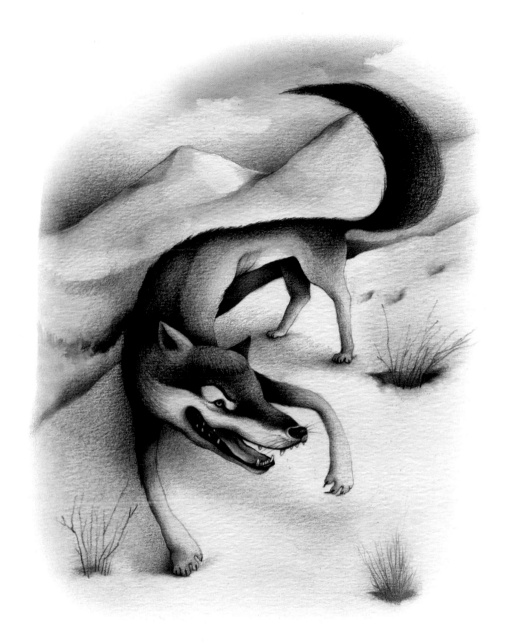

MORAL

Do not pretend to be something

that you are not.

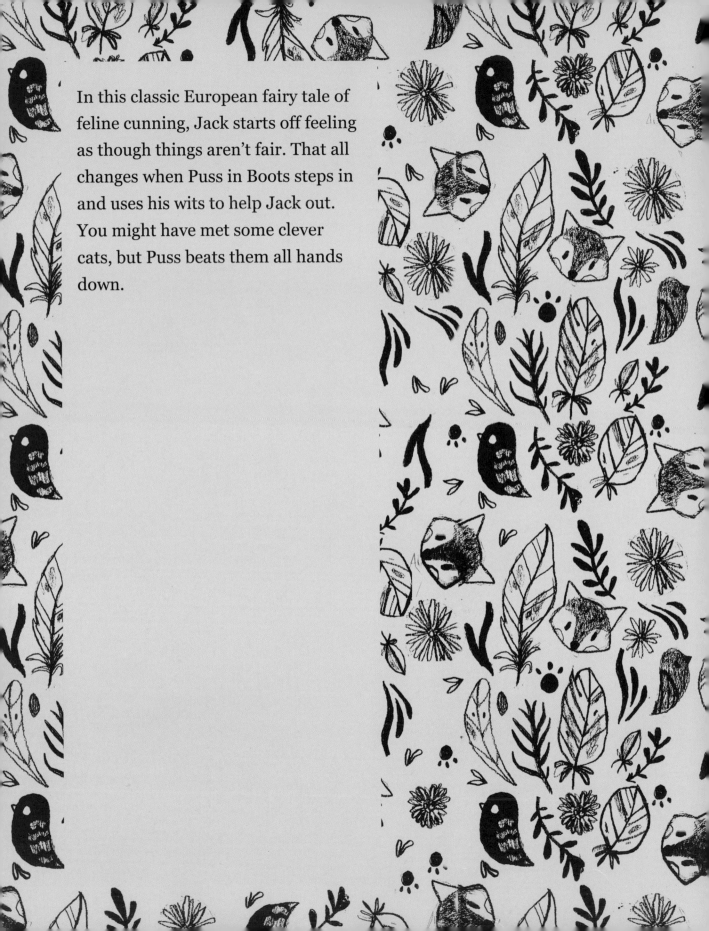

In this classic European fairy tale of feline cunning, Jack starts off feeling as though things aren't fair. That all changes when Puss in Boots steps in and uses his wits to help Jack out. You might have met some clever cats, but Puss beats them all hands down.

Puss in Boots

Retold by Pippa Goodhart

Illustrated by Thomas Radcliffe

An old miller died, leaving his mill to his eldest son. He left his donkey to his middle son, and the cat to his youngest son, Jack.

"We two older ones will work together," said the oldest son. "We can make flour at the mill. Then we can take the flour to market on the donkey. We don't need a cat. Goodbye, Jack!"

"That's not fair!" said Jack. "What am I supposed to do with a cat? You will be rich and I will be poor. That's not fair at all!"

"Bad luck," said his brothers.

But Jack didn't know that his cat wasn't an ordinary cat. His cat was the one and only Puss in Boots. Puss didn't just wear boots. He could talk. He said, "No other cat is as clever as me. I will make you rich! Just wait and see!"

Puss took a basket. He went
to a field and he threw down grains
of corn. Then Puss hid. Rabbits came
to nibble the corn, and—*trap!*—Puss
caught three rabbits.

Puss in Boots gave Jack one rabbit to cook for their supper.

"I might not be rich, but at least we will eat well tonight," said Jack. "Thank you, Puss."

While Jack was busy chopping onions, Puss took the other two rabbits down the road to the king's palace.

Puss in Boots *knock knocked* at the palace door. It was opened by the king himself. Puss in Boots bowed very low.

"Your marvelous Majesty, here is a present from my master," he said.

"Oh, how kind," said the king. "Tell me, who is your master?"

"My master is the marquis of Carabas," said Puss in Boots.

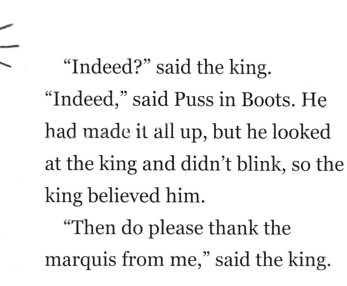

"Indeed?" said the king.
"Indeed," said Puss in Boots. He
had made it all up, but he looked
at the king and didn't blink, so the
king believed him.

"Then do please thank the
marquis from me," said the king.

Puss in Boots purred as he and Jack ate their rabbit stew. "This is all very nice," said Jack. "But I would still like to be rich, you know."

"Ah, master, you must learn to trust me," said Puss. "I *will* still make you rich. Just wait and see."

The next day, Puss in Boots set another trap. This
time he caught four partridges.

"Roast partridge for supper," said Jack. "And
maybe some partridge feathers to stuff my pillow? I
may not be rich, but at least I will be comfortable."

While Jack was cooking supper, Puss in Boots walked down the road to the king's palace once again. *Knock knock.*

"Hello. I remember you, Puss," said the king.

"Your marvelous Majesty," said Puss in Boots, bowing low. "Here is another present from the marquis of Carabas."

"Goodness, he *is* kind!" said the king, taking the partridges.

The day after that, Jack and Puss in Boots were walking down the road, when Puss said to Jack, "Quick! Take off your clothes and get into the river."

"What?" said Jack. "Why should I?"

"You must just trust me. Do as I say. Then wait and see what happens," said Puss.

So Jack took off his clothes
and jumped into the river—*splash!*
Puss hid Jack's clothes behind a rock.
"Hey!" shouted Jack angrily.
"Shush!" said Puss. "Here comes the king!"
He was right. The king's coach was coming
along the road.
"Splash around in the water," Puss told Jack.
So Jack splashed.

Puss in Boots ran into the road. He waved his paws. "Stop!" he shouted. "Oh, please help me!" he said, as the king put his head out of the window. "My master, the marquis of Carabas, was swimming in the river when somebody stole his clothes! Now he can't get out of the river because he has nothing to wear!"

"Goodness!" said the king. "Stop the coach at once!
The marquis of Carabas has been so kind to me, I must
help him. He can wear some of my clothes. Unpack them
from my box!"

The king's footman handed fine clothes to Puss, and
Puss handed them to Jack.

Jack quickly got dressed. Then he stepped forward.

"Thank you for the clothes," he said. And Puss

pushed him to make him bow down low.

"Not at all," said the king. "Not at all."

Jack looked very handsome in the royal clothes.
The king's daughter noticed that. The king told his
daughter, "Princess Sophia, my dear, this young man is
the marquis of Carabas. He has been so kind, giving me
presents. We must give him a lift in our coach."

"Yes, I agree," said Princess Sophia.

So the king and the princess and Jack got into the
coach, and they set off down the road.

Where was Puss in Boots? He ran ahead of the
coach. Why? Because he had a clever plan. Wait
and see!

There were people harvesting a fine crop of wheat in the fields. Puss ran over to them. He looked at the people fiercely and said, "The king is coming! If he asks who owns all this land, tell him that it belongs to the marquis of Carabas. If you don't, I'll lose my temper with you!" And Puss showed them his claws.

Soon the king's coach came by. The king called from his coach window, "Tell me, good people, whose fine land is this?"

They all replied, "It belongs to the marquis of Carabas, Your Majesty."

"Does it indeed!" said the king. *Goodness*, he thought. *This marquis is a rich man.* And he gave Jack a smile.

83

Up ahead was a very grand castle. Puss knew that the castle belonged to a terrible ogre. But Puss, being Puss, had a clever and cunning plan that was going to make Jack a very rich man.

While the king was talking to the people in the field,
Puss in Boots arrived at the castle door. *Knock knock.*
The ogre opened the door.

"What do you want?"
roared the ogre's big
mouth full of teeth.

"Oh, marvelous Mr. Ogre, sir," said Puss, bowing low. "I have heard such wonderful things about you! Now I have come to see for myself if what they say is true."

"Wonderful things?" roared the ogre, pulling Puss inside. "What wonderful things have you heard about me, pussy cat?"

"Well," said Puss. "I did hear that you can magic yourself into something even bigger than you already are." Puss shook his head. "But I didn't believe it."

"Oh, but I can!" said the ogre. "Watch this!" The ogre turned himself into a huge, snarly lion! Puss in Boots ran up the curtains to get away.

"That's all very well," said Puss from up high. "But turning into something big must be easy for a big ogre like you. I bet you can't make yourself really small."

"Oh yes, I can!" said the ogre. And he shrank into a tiny little mouse.

Down jumped Puss, and—*pounce!*
Puss in Boots ate that ogre mouse . . .
just in time, because somebody was
knocking at the castle door.

Knock knock.

"Ah, your marvelous Majesty!" said Puss in Boots,
opening the door and bowing low. "Welcome to the home
of the marquis of Carabas!"

"Really?" said Jack.

"Really," said Puss in Boots firmly.

"Goodness," said the king.

Can you guess what happened not very long after that?

90

Princess Sophia and Jack got married. Jack's big brothers came to the royal wedding on their donkey. And guess what they said when they saw Jack with his princess and his castle? They said, "That's not fair!"

"Bad luck," said Jack.
Purrrrr . . . went Puss in Boots.

In this fable from Africa, Baboon is a mischief-maker like some of the characters we've met already in this collection. But in this story, Baboon gets his comeuppance, because he falls for a trick himself! Do you like it when the trickster gets away with it, or do you think they deserve their punishment?

The Tortoise and the Baboon

Retold by Timothy Knapman

Illustrated by Linda Selby

Baboon thought it was funny to play tricks on others. One afternoon, he saw Tortoise walking along. Tortoise was going so slowly that he gave Baboon an idea.

"My dear old friend," said Baboon. "Goodness me, you're looking thin!"

"That's because I couldn't find anything to eat today," said Tortoise gloomily.

"Then you must come and have supper with me," said Baboon. "I've got plenty of food and I'm a very good cook. Giraffe is always coming over and you know what a fussy eater he is."

"Thank you, Baboon," said Tortoise.

Baboon scampered off to get things ready.

It took poor Tortoise ages to get to Baboon's home. The path was long and knobbly and a lot of it was uphill.

More than once Tortoise thought about giving up. Then he remembered the food Baboon had promised him and that gave him the strength to go on.

"I'm sorry I'm late," said Tortoise, when he finally arrived.

"Not to worry," said Baboon. "There it is: A feast fit for a king!"

Baboon pointed up to the treetops. Three large baskets, full of scrumptious food, hung from the highest branches.

"I can't reach them!" said Tortoise. "Please, Baboon, will you bring something down for me?"

"I suppose you'll want me to cut it up and feed it to you as well!" snorted the Baboon. "No, no. If you want the food, you must get it for yourself. Giraffe said it was easy."

Tortoise realized he'd been tricked. He was hungry and tired and a long, long way from home.

Baboon laughed for days afterward. When his friends told him he'd been cruel, Baboon said, "Oh, Tortoise doesn't mind."

You are invited
to tea
this afternoon
at . . .
Tortoise's house.

Then a card arrived from Tortoise, inviting Baboon to tea.

"I told you he's a good sport," said Baboon.

Sure enough, when Baboon arrived at Tortoise's home, the table was piled high with cakes. Tortoise was already starting to eat and called out, "Please come and join me."

Now this was during the dry season, when the sun is so hot that the countryside can catch fire easily. Between Baboon and Tortoise was a patch of grass that had been scorched black in a bush fire. Baboon went bounding across it to the table, but just as he was reaching out for a cake, Tortoise said, "Where are your manners? Don't you know you should wash your hands first?"

Baboon looked at his hands. Tortoise was right; they
were filthy from bounding across the blackened grass.

"I'm terribly sorry," said Baboon. He went and washed his hands in the river, but because he had to cross the blackened grass to get back, his hands were all dirty again by the time he reached the table.

"It's no good, Baboon," said Tortoise, cramming his mouth with cake. "I can't give you any food until your hands are clean."

That wretched Baboon went back and forth to the river all afternoon, but each time he came back to the table his hands were filthy and Tortoise wouldn't give him any food.

Finally, when he had eaten up every last cake, and Baboon had eaten nothing, Tortoise said, "I hope you've learned your lesson."

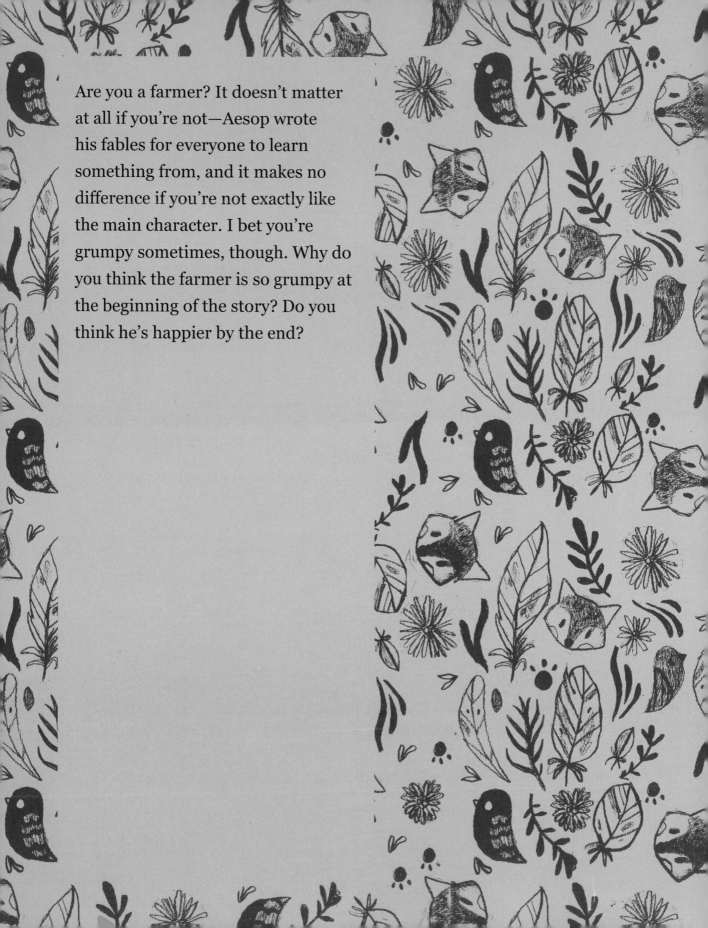

Are you a farmer? It doesn't matter at all if you're not—Aesop wrote his fables for everyone to learn something from, and it makes no difference if you're not exactly like the main character. I bet you're grumpy sometimes, though. Why do you think the farmer is so grumpy at the beginning of the story? Do you think he's happier by the end?

The Farmer and the Eagle

Retold by Joanna Nadin

Illustrated by Irina Troitskaya

In a land far away there lived a farmer. He was a grumpy man who had little time for people or animals.

"People will trick you," he said to himself. "And animals are food, not friends."

Instead, he worked long and hard,
whatever the weather.

He plowed the land.

He milked the cows.

He took the sheep to market.

Any animal who tried to steal from the farmer was in for a nasty surprise because he set nets to keep them out.

Every day he would check the nets, muttering to himself as he went.

"Wretched rabbits, chomping on my lettuces."

And if he caught one, he would take it home and eat it for a snack.

But one day he found a golden eagle had become tangled in one of his nets.

"Help me," she cried. "I'm stuck."

Now the farmer didn't like eagles because they stole lambs. But this bird was so majestic that he found himself cutting the net and setting her free.

Later, he was annoyed by his mercy. "She'll probably rob me," he grumbled.

For many weeks after, he saw the eagle flying high above him as he worked.

"Go away," he would snap. But she didn't go away.

Summer came, and the days grew longer and hotter. One afternoon, the farmer settled himself against an old stone wall for a rest.

"Just a snooze," he said to himself. "There's still work to be done."

He was so tired he didn't see that the stones were teetering and threatening to tumble.

But someone did.

The farmer woke with a start to find the eagle
flapping around his head and screeching.

"Get off!" he yelled. "Go away."

But the eagle wouldn't go away. Instead, she snatched
his hat and flew off with it. The farmer leaped up to
snatch it back.

"Stop, thief!" he called.

Well, the eagle didn't stop and the farmer couldn't catch her. He stomped back to the stone wall to collect his things.

But when he got there, he found nothing
but a pile of rocks.

"I would have died," he exclaimed, "if the eagle hadn't saved me."

And since that day, the farmer and the eagle call out to each other as they work.

"Hello, Man," she cries.

And the farmer waves back. "Hello, Friend."

So now, if the eagle finds a lost lamb, she carries it back to him.

And if the farmer catches a rabbit in his net, he leaves it out for her snack.

And he eats a cheese sandwich instead.

MORAL
One good turn
deserves another.

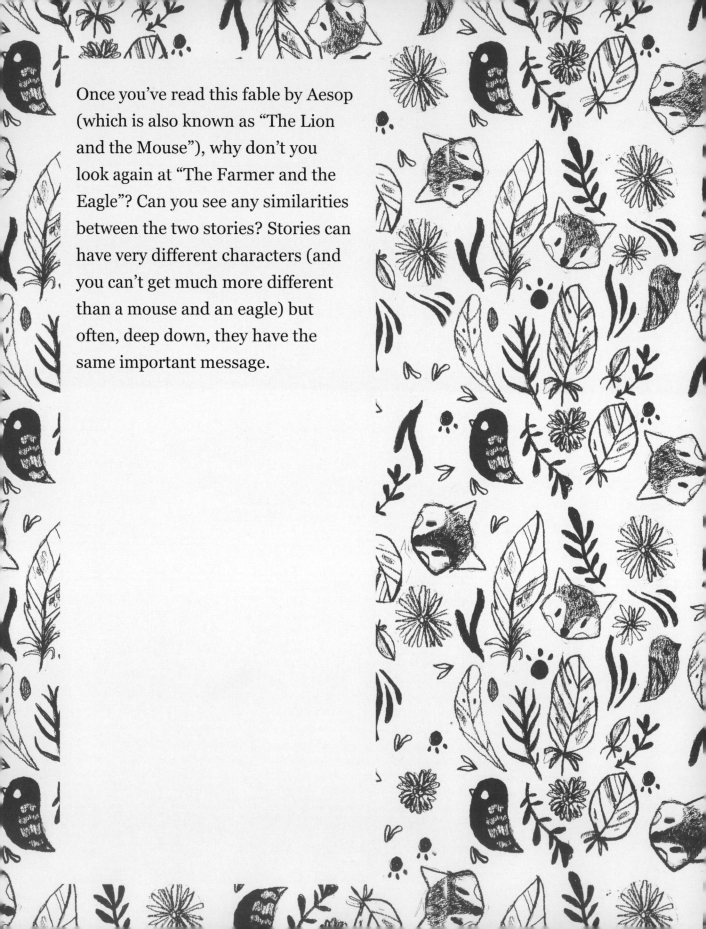

Once you've read this fable by Aesop (which is also known as "The Lion and the Mouse"), why don't you look again at "The Farmer and the Eagle"? Can you see any similarities between the two stories? Stories can have very different characters (and you can't get much more different than a mouse and an eagle) but often, deep down, they have the same important message.

Let
Me Go

Retold by Geraldine McCaughrean

Illustrated by Alex Wilson
and David Pavon

Lions are a lazy group. They spend long hours sleeping in the sun. They even send their wives out to do the hunting for them. So it was an easy mistake to make. Little Mouse thought it was safe to creep past the giant paws, the long, damp nose, the closed eyes, the wiry whiskers. But Big Lion was not asleep.

Gotcha!

One paw came down—*thud*—on poor Little Mouse, and knocked her flat. The other paw scooped her toward an open mouth.

"Wait! Wait! Please! Don't eat me! I am too small to do you good. At home I have twenty-two mouslings! You are King of Beasts and royalty shouldn't sink to cruelty!"

"I am a cat," said Big Lion. "Cats eat mice." And he rolled Little Mouse between the black, scratchy pads of both front paws.

"Oh, but such a cat! Greatest of all cats! They call you King of the Jungle, and kings should be wise, gracious, merciful, and large of spirit! I confess that I am the smallest and least important creature in your kingdom, but let me live, and one day I may do you some great service!"

Big Lion gave a throaty laugh that smelled of raw meat. "What could you ever do for me, absurd rodent? Mice are too small ever to be useful."

Just then, he caught sight of his wife dragging a dead gazelle home from hunting. He would eat well, no matter what, and he had liked those words: "gracious," "merciful," and "large of spirit." So he let Little Mouse go, and watched her speed over the ground as fast as the shadow of a wren. Before she was even out of sight, she was forgotten.

But Little Mouse
did not forget.

Hunters more fearful than lionesses were hunting the plains of the Oko Vanga: poachers!

One sweltering day, Lion lay down in the shade of a tree. Something dropped out of the branches overhead—something without a smell or even a shape. It smothered Lion in lines and loops and, when he tried to escape, tangled itself even more tightly around him.

A poacher's net.

Soon Lion lay
knotted, helpless, and—
do not speak it out loud—very
scared indeed. Strength could not
burst the net, cunning could not free him;
his lionesses had fled. A noise escaped Lion rather
like kittens mewing.

"I will free you, Your Majesty," said a little voice.

"Oh, Little Mouse, nothing can save me now
from the poachers' knives," moaned Big Lion.

Little Mouse had tiny teeth. She began to nibble at the cords of the net. Such tiny teeth, such coarse and hairy rope, but Little Mouse nibbled and spat, nibbled and spat, until there was a hole the size of a paw, a hole the size of a nose.

The ground rumbled like hunger. The poachers were coming back. But still Little Mouse nibbled and spat, nibbled and spat, until there was a hole the size of a lion's head, a lion's mane. Out through the hole came the head and behind it came the rest of the King of Beasts, in a flailing scramble to be free.

Both Lion and Mouse set off to run. They did not run in the same direction, of course: Mice and lions do not make good neighbors.

But sometimes little acts of kindness are remembered for a lifetime. For the rest of her tiny, timorous life, Little Mouse never forgot Big Lion, who had spared her life. For the rest of his fierce and furry life, Big Lion never forgot Little Mouse, or the day she had saved his life.

Anansi the Spider is one of the most important characters in West African and Caribbean folklore. He is the ultimate trickster, and is never short of ideas for having fun, usually at the expense of other creatures. But mischievous characters aren't always the baddies. Just look at Anansi, whose tricks on this occasion help his friends get out of a very scary situation.

Anansi and the Antelope Baby

Retold by Tony Bradman

Illustrated by Steve Horrocks

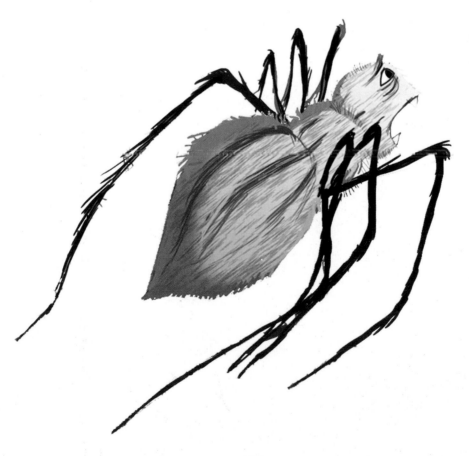

Everybody has heard about Anansi the Spider and his tricks, of course. He's the eight-legged King of Mischief with a reputation for playing pranks. But even he needs some help from time to time—and that's when you might get to see he has a decent side to his character, too.

One day, he was hanging around in a bush, spinning a web, as spiders do. Anansi was thinking about all the tricks he might play when suddenly he smelled smoke. He scrambled to the top of the bush to find out what was going on and his eyes nearly popped out. The forest was on fire and a wall of flames was heading his way!

"Oh no, I'm in big trouble now!" Anansi muttered to himself. "My little legs will never outrun that fire. What can I do?"

All the animals in the forest were running away. Anansi called out to each one as they rushed past, "Help me, please!" but none of them did as he asked.

Anansi didn't have many friends because of all the

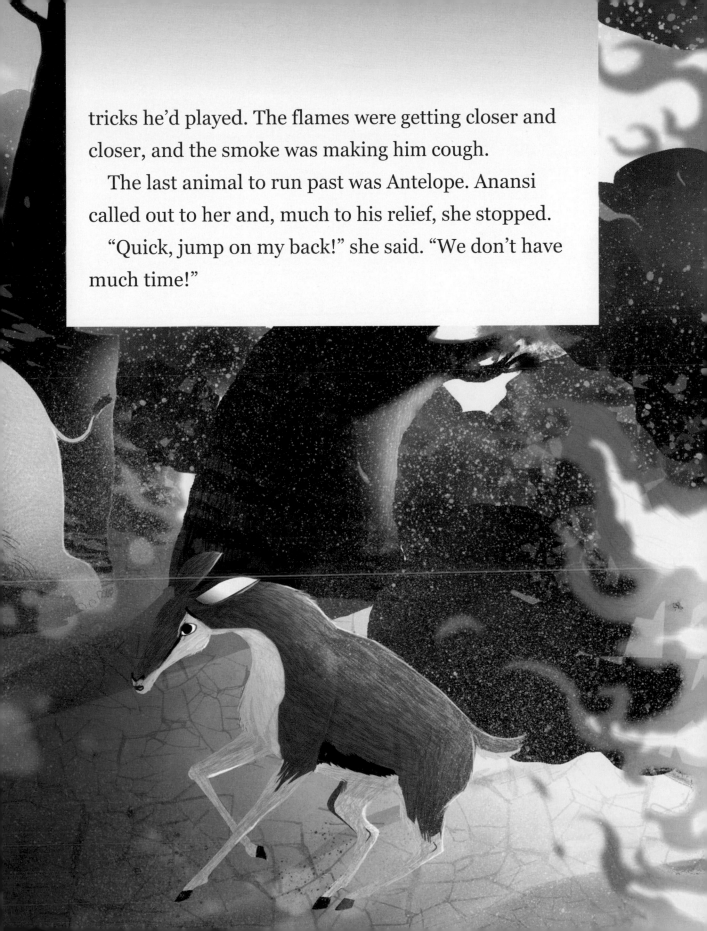

tricks he'd played. The flames were getting closer and closer, and the smoke was making him cough.

The last animal to run past was Antelope. Anansi called out to her and, much to his relief, she stopped.

"Quick, jump on my back!" she said. "We don't have much time!"

Anansi didn't need to be told twice.
He leaped onto her back and she ran off, her long legs
flying over the ground. Anansi hung on as he bounced
up and down.

The flames were just behind them, and he thought
they weren't going to make it, but they did. They
reached the edge of the forest where the fire stopped.

"Phew, that was close!"
said Anansi, lowering
himself to the ground.
"I can't thank you
enough, Antelope. If you
ever need any help, you can
certainly count on me."

"That's very kind of you,
Anansi," said Antelope. "Take
care of yourself—goodbye!"

Anansi watched her go, then went on his way himself.

Time passed and things settled down again. The forest started growing, all the animals came back, and Anansi got up to his usual mischief. But he had a soft spot for Antelope and never tried any tricks on her or her new baby—a beautiful little creature she clearly adored.

One day, Anansi was hanging around in a tree when he saw the two of them.

"You stay here, Baby," Anansi heard Antelope say, as she tucked him under a bush. "I'm going to get some of that sweet grass you love. Don't worry, I won't be long."

Then she bounded off. Anansi turned to leave, but then he saw two hunters come out from behind a nearby rock! Anansi hid behind the tree so they wouldn't spot him.

"Come on, after her!" said the first hunter. "We can return for the baby later."

Anansi watched them go and felt worried about his friend. He decided she would probably be all right, though—she could run like the wind and had escaped hunters before. But what if she kept going, thinking she was leading them away from Baby? The hunters would just give up the chase and come back for him.

Anansi realized that only *he* could save Baby—but what could he do? Anansi desperately racked his brains . . . and at last, it came to him.

What if he spun a web around the bush so the hunters couldn't see Baby?

Anansi quickly got to work, but the hunters came back before he'd finished. Anansi stopped what he was doing and watched them nervously from behind a leaf. They looked rather annoyed, so Anansi guessed Antelope had escaped.

"Where's the baby?" said the first hunter. "This was the place, wasn't it?"

"Yes, I thought he was under this bush," said the second hunter. "Although it looks different now—it didn't have this spider web on it."

"You're right," said the first hunter. "But let's have a closer look . . ."

Anansi felt a surge of panic—he had to finish the web! He started spinning as fast as he could, keeping one step ahead of them as they walked around the bush.

It was touch and go . . . but he got the whole bush

covered just in time. Then he lowered himself to the ground beside Baby and waited, holding his breath.

"No, this can't be the same bush," said the first hunter at last.

"Come on then," said the second hunter. "Let's look elsewhere."

141

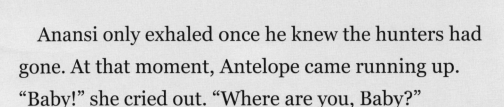

Anansi only exhaled once he knew the hunters had gone. At that moment, Antelope came running up. "Baby!" she cried out. "Where are you, Baby?"

"Don't worry, Antelope," said Anansi, tugging a hole in the web. "Here he is!"

Anansi told Antelope what had happened and she was very relieved.

"Oh, Anansi," she said. "I'll never be able to thank you enough!"

"Think nothing of it," said Anansi. "That's what friends are for."

The other animals didn't believe it when Antelope told them he'd said that . . .

But for once, the King of Mischief really, really meant it!

Have you ever been in a tricky situation and thought, "What I could really use right now is a magical talking cow?" If not, things are about to change! This poetic adventure will make you feel as though you're in the distant mountains of Iceland with Frida and her beautiful cow, Bukolla.

The Magic Cow

Retold by Claire Llewellyn

Illustrated by Anaïs Goldemberg

Once upon a time in Iceland, there lived a poor husband and wife. They had a small farm in the mountains where they lived with their daughter, Frida.

The couple kept a beautiful brown cow called Bukolla. Twice a day, the wife milked Bukolla. Twice a day, the rich, creamy milk filled the bucket to the brim. How the couple loved that cow! To tell the truth, they loved her more than their own child.

One morning, the woman went to milk Bukolla. To her horror, the barn was empty. The cow was gone!

"Husband, husband, Bukolla's gone!" she cried.

The two of them searched all day for the cow, but they could not find her anywhere.

That night, the couple were in an awful mood.

"Frida," snapped her mother, "tomorrow you must go into the mountains and look for Bukolla."

"And don't come back until you find her!" growled her father.

Early the next morning, Frida set off along the path that led into the hills. She was wearing a new pair of red leather shoes. On her back, she carried a bag of bread and cheese.

The path led Frida through a grassy meadow. Then it began to go uphill.

It twisted and turned around large rocks. It crossed a fast-flowing stream.

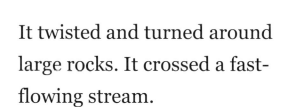

After an hour, Frida grew tired. She sat on a rock and ate some bread and cheese.

She decided to call to the missing cow.

Bukolla! Can you hear me, my dear?
Moo to me if you're somewhere near.

Far, far away, Frida heard a faint "Moo."
She jumped up and started walking toward it.

151

As Frida climbed higher and higher,
the hills grew wilder and wilder. A
waterfall poured over dark, gloomy
rocks. Ice lay here and there on
the path. After an hour, the girl
began to tire. She sat down
on a patch of grass and ate
more bread and cheese.

For a second time, she called out to the cow.

Once again she heard a "Moo." This time, it sounded louder. She jumped up and headed toward it.

Higher and higher Frida climbed. The sky grew dark with clouds and a cold wind began to blow. The girl shivered and hugged herself to keep out the chill. After an hour, she was tired again, so she sat down on a rock to rest.

For a third time, Frida called out.

This time, she heard a very loud "Moo," which seemed to come from under her feet! Was Bukolla stuck in a cave somewhere? Frida jumped up and looked around.

Frida saw a wide opening in a
rock nearby. She went through
and followed a track that led
down into a large cave. Her brave
heart gave a leap. Bukolla, the
beautiful brown cow, was tied to a
ring in the wall!

Now, Frida was a smart girl. She knew all about the wicked trolls that live in mountain caves. So she quickly untied Bukolla. Then she led the cow back through the opening and the two of them turned for home.

The cloudy sky was darker still as Frida and Bukolla hurried back along the path. They had not gone far when they heard angry voices. Frida turned and saw two women behind her. They were the strangest women she had ever seen. One was huge and the other was tiny. Both were ugly, fierce, and strong. Frida knew at once that they were trolls. And they were coming after her and Bukolla!

Frida was shaking from head to toe. She
cried, "Oh, Bukolla, what can we do?"

Then, wonder of wonders, the cow spoke.

Pluck a hair
from my tail, dear
girl, and lay it
on the ground.

Frida plucked one of Bukolla's brown
hairs and laid it on the path.

The magic cow looked at the hair. She said,

Hair, turn into a river so wide
That only a bird can cross to
the other side.

Instantly, a huge river blocked the
path between Frida and the trolls.

When the tiny troll saw the river, she stamped her foot in anger.

But the big troll said, "I have an idea. Go back and fetch our best bull, and be quick about it."

In a moment, the tiny troll was back with a magnificent black bull.

Her big sister led the bull to the river and the beast began to drink. It drank and drank until the river was dry.

Frida and Bukolla were halfway home when they heard voices again. Frida turned and saw the two angry trolls. They were getting closer and closer. The girl's teeth were chattering with fear. She cried, "Oh, Bukolla, what can we do?"

Bukolla said,

Pluck a hair from my tail, dear girl, and lay it on the ground.

Frida plucked another hair from the long brown tail. The magic cow said to the hair,

Hair, turn into a fire so vast
That only a bird could ever
get past.

Instantly, a great fire blocked the path between Frida and the trolls.

163

The tiny troll was very angry and shook her fist at the blazing fire.

But her big sister said, "I have an idea. Hurry back along the path and bring back the black bull. Sister, be quick!"

In a flash, the troll came back with the bull. The magnificent beast had drunk a river and was about to burst.

And burst it did!

Water poured all over the fire and soon the fire was out.

Frida was nearly home when she heard angry voices again. She turned and saw the trolls behind her on the path.

She cried, "Oh, Bukolla, what can we do?"

For a third time, Bukolla said,

> Pluck a hair from my tail, dear girl, and lay it on the ground.

Frida plucked a long brown
hair and laid it on the grass.

The magic cow said to the hair,

> Hair, turn into a mountain so high
> That only a bird can pass you by.

At that instant, a mighty
mountain blocked the path
between Frida and the trolls.

The smaller troll
howled with rage when
she saw the mountain.
But her big sister said,
"I have an idea. Run to
our cave as fast as you can
and bring back hammers
and picks."

The tiny troll did as she was told. In the blink of an eye, she came back. She was carrying the hammers and picks.

Then the sisters began to tunnel through the rock. Their tunnel got deeper and deeper, and smaller and smaller . . . until the walls were so tight that the trolls got stuck! They could not move forward. They could not move back.

They shouted and cried, but it made no difference. And that is where they stay to this very day.

So Frida and Bukolla arrived home safely. Frida's parents greeted them warmly. They were delighted to see their cow.

They were quite pleased to see Frida, too.

169

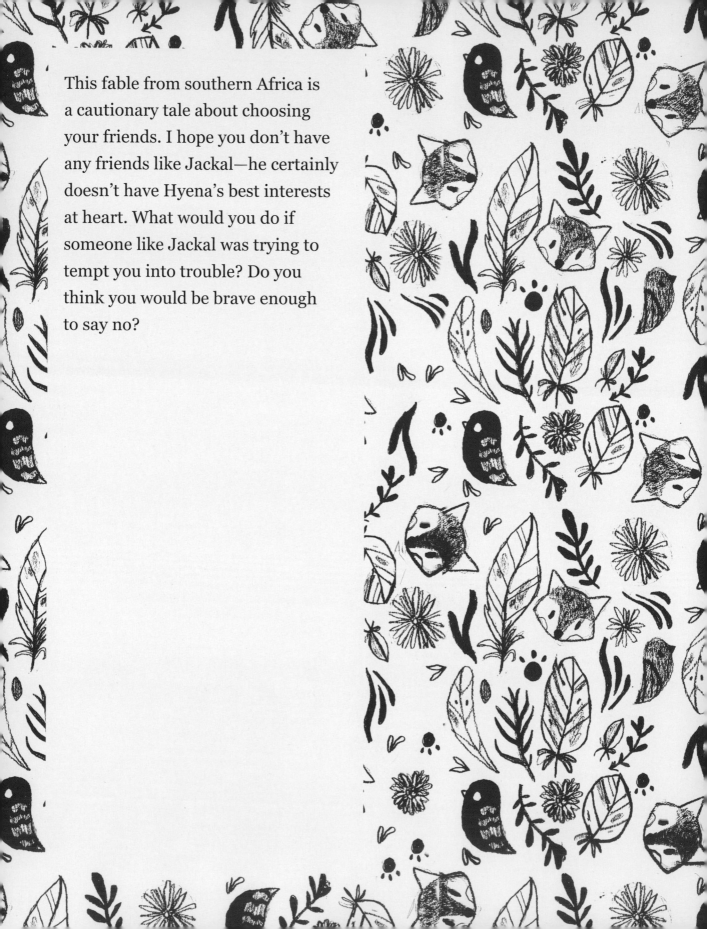

This fable from southern Africa is a cautionary tale about choosing your friends. I hope you don't have any friends like Jackal—he certainly doesn't have Hyena's best interests at heart. What would you do if someone like Jackal was trying to tempt you into trouble? Do you think you would be brave enough to say no?

The Hungry Hyena

Retold by Timothy Knapman

Illustrated by Linda Selby

Hyena hadn't eaten for a week and his stomach was making the most extraordinary noises.

He watched the other animals going by, with their shiny eyes and their glossy coats, and felt so sorry for himself.

"Hyena, my dear fellow," said Jackal, "why so glum?"

Before Hyena could answer, his stomach went *squisheronk-squerat-squoot!*

"Tummy rumbling, is it?" said Jackal. "Why didn't you say? I've just found the most amazing place to eat. It's over where the men live, so we'll have to be careful."

That evening, Jackal took Hyena to a pen with a tall fence around it.

"You see in there?" said Jackal. "There are sheep and there are goats. You can have as many sheep as you like, but don't touch the goats. They make a noise if you bite them, and that will get the dogs barking, and before you know it the men will be after us with their clubs!"

"How do we get in?" said Hyena.

"I wondered when you were going to ask that," said Jackal. "Follow me."

Jackal led Hyena to a secret place where there was a hole in the fence. It wasn't very big so they had to breathe in and squeeze up, but at last they got through.

Hyena grabbed one of the sheep. He was so hungry he swallowed it down in a single gulp. Then he had another and another until his stomach hung so far down beneath him it actually scraped along the ground!

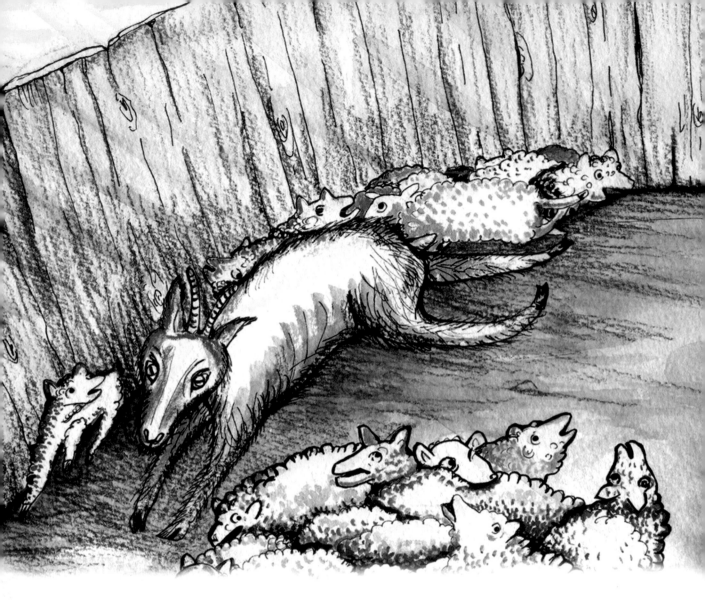

"I won't get through the fence if I keep going like
this," said Hyena.

"Go on, just one more," said Jackal. "Hurry, though.
Soon it'll be sunrise and the men will be on their way."

They were just waddling over to the hole in the fence
when Jackal saw a particularly tasty-looking goat.

"What are you doing?" said Hyena.

"One bite can't do any harm," replied Jackal.

"I thought you said—"

Too late! Jackal was so tempted that he ignored his own advice and sank his teeth into the goat's shoulder.

The goat gave a terrible shriek and at once the dogs started barking.

"Oops!" said Jackal. "Quick! Before the men get here!"

The two of them dashed over to the hole in the fence. Jackal just about wriggled through, but Hyena was now so large with all the food he had eaten, he got stuck.

"Help!" cried Hyena.

"Sorry, pal," said Jackal. "It's what I planned all along. The men will be so busy punishing you, they'll never catch me!" He raced off as fast as he could go.

Hyena struggled with all his might, but it was no good. He was trapped. The men were coming and they were very angry.

As he curled up later, alone and miserable, Hyena had quite forgotten the delicious feast he'd enjoyed only a few hours before.

He swore he'd be more careful when he chose his friends in the future.

MORAL

Beware of friends you
can't trust.

Aesop wrote over seven hundred fables in his lifetime—can you imagine how many bookshelves he must have had? It's amazing that his stories still have something to teach us today. "The Fox and the Crow" has lots of lessons within it: that sometimes tricksters have tricks played back on them, how vanity can lead you to lose your treats, and how being jealous of someone else's treat doesn't always end well. What else does the story make you think about?

The Fox
and the Crow

Retold by Joanna Nadin

Illustrated by Irina Troitskaya

One fine day, Fox came across a fat piece of meat behind the butcher's shop.

He licked his lips. "What a lucky fox I am," he said. "But I'm full from my lunch right now. I shall save this meat for my dinner." So he picked it up carefully and trotted home with it between his teeth.

But the journey was quite
long and Fox was tired by the
time he arrived.
"Maybe I'll just have a little
nap," he said.

And that is just what he did.
He yawned and stretched and
settled down under a tree, with
the meat safely by his side.

Zzzzzz

Or so he thought.

Because while Fox slept, Crow landed on a branch and spied the meat. He also saw that Fox was fast asleep.

"Silly old Fox," said Crow to himself. "I shall snatch that meat and fly high up where he can't reach me."

And that is just what he did.

Fox woke up to find his meat missing.

"Where could it have gone?" he said.

He looked to the left, but he couldn't see it.

He looked to the right, but he couldn't see it.

And then he looked up and saw Crow with the meat dangling from his beak.

How very rude, thought Fox. *But I shall teach Crow a lesson.*

Now Fox knew that Crow was very vain and liked to be flattered.

"Oh, Crow," he said. "What a fine-looking fellow you are."

Crow smiled to himself, for it was true; he was, indeed, a fine-looking fellow.

"Oh, Crow," said Fox again. "You are truly a bird fit to be king of all creatures."

Crow smiled to himself, for it was true; he was, indeed, a bird fit to be king of all creatures.

Then Fox played his trick.

"It is a shame," he said, "that your voice is so out of tune."

With those words, Crow became very insulted. Him, a bird fit to be king of all creatures, out of tune? There was only one thing to do: he would have to prove Fox wrong.

So he opened his beak nice and wide to sing his favorite song.

But as he did so, the meat fell out and dropped straight into the mouth of Fox, who swallowed it down in one gulp.

Crow cawed angrily as he realized he had been tricked and that his vanity got the better of him.

"I shall never let myself be flattered again," he said.

And he *almost* never did.

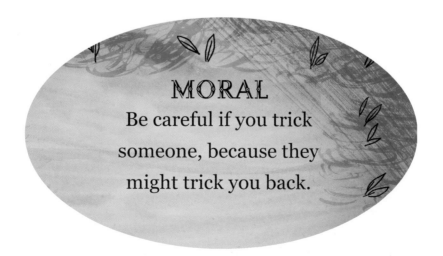

MORAL
Be careful if you trick
someone, because they
might trick you back.

Not all stories have to have a clear moral at the end of them. Some are really fun to read or hear just because they're great stories. "The King of Cats" is a spooky folk tale that comes from Britain, and was first written about 500 years ago. It doesn't offer any explanation to what is going on, and that adds to its uncanny mood. Cats are often connected to the supernatural—why do you think that is?

The King
of Cats

Retold by Elizabeth Laird

Illustrated by Yannick Robert

In the old, old days of long-ago Britain, people were a little bit afraid of cats. They thought that cats had strange powers.

"You want to be careful around cats," they would say. "They know a bit too much about death, and the underworld, and things that might happen in the future."

Here's one of the stories they liked to tell.

One dark night, an old woman sat beside her fire. Tom, her cat, sat beside her. His green eyes were closed.

It was a stormy night. The wind was howling around the house and making the windows rattle.

"Are you asleep, Tom?" asked the old woman. But the cat didn't move a whisker.

The old woman's husband, Peter the gravedigger, was out in the churchyard. Suddenly, he ran into the cottage. His hair was standing on end, and his eyes were round with fear.

"What's the matter with you?" said his wife.

"I was digging a grave," said Peter. "But I was so tired, I think my mind started playing tricks on me. Suddenly, I heard a cat say, *Meow!*"

"Meow!" echoed Tom from his corner.

"Well," the gravedigger went on, "I looked up, and I saw such a sight!"

He stopped and wiped his head with his handkerchief.

"What sight?" said his wife impatiently. "What are you talking about?"

"It was a procession of cats," said the gravedigger. "Nine of them there were, all black, like Tom here.

And they were carrying a little coffin. And all the time they were saying, *Meow!*"

"Meow!" said Tom again.

"And on the coffin was a red velvet cushion, with a tiny crown of gold sitting on it. Why, look at our Tom! He's staring at me with great big eyes. Do you think he understands what I'm saying?"

"Oh, you silly man," said his wife. "Go on with your silly story."

"Well, the cats were all crying out together, *Meow! Meow!*—"

"Meow!" sang out Tom.

"Yes, just like that. Then one of them came right up to me and he said—"

"What do you mean, he *said*?" said his wife. "Cats can't speak!"

"Well, this one could," said Peter. "He said, 'Go and tell Tom Tildrum that Tim Toldrum's dead.'"

"What nonsense!" his wife said. "I don't believe a word of it. I think you'd better get yourself to bed for an early night."

But the gravedigger didn't move. He was staring at their cat.

Tom was growing in front of their eyes.

He was swelling up like a balloon, and his great green eyes were shining like lamps. He jumped to his four black feet, and lashed his long black tail. Then he cried out, "Tim Toldrum's dead, is he? Then I'm the King of Cats!"

Then, to their astonishment, Tom leaped over the fire and ran up the chimney. And that was the last the gravedigger and his wife ever saw of him.

A collection of greatest animal stories wouldn't be complete without a retelling of the story of Noah's ark. Have you ever wondered how the animals got along with each other once they were all on the ark together? This version thinks about some of the smaller animals and how they came to be. Which animals would you focus on if you were telling the story of Noah's ark?

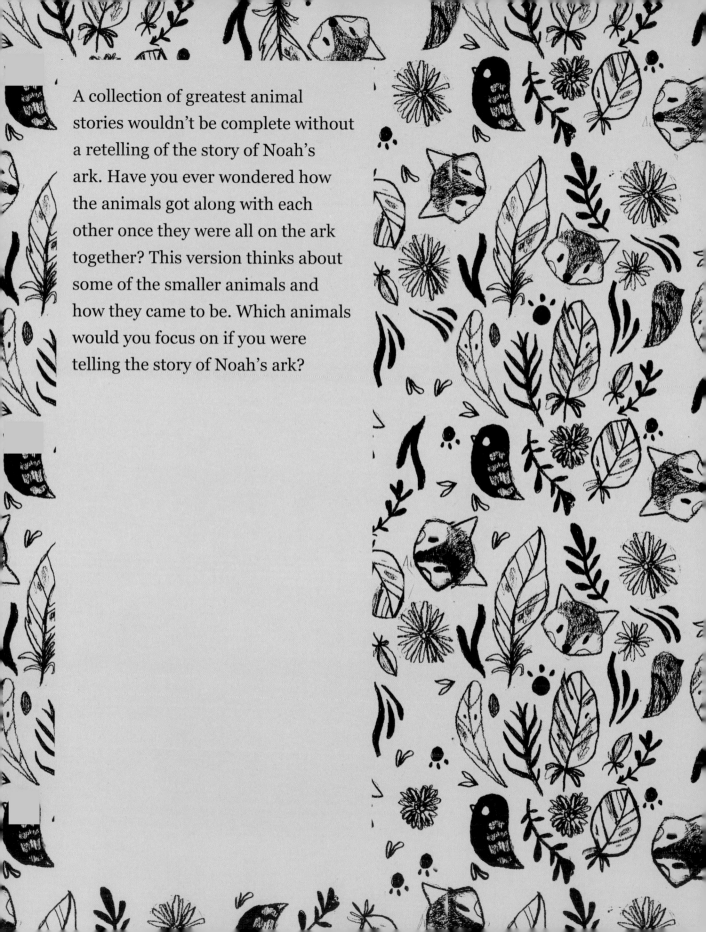

All
Aboard

Retold by Geraldine McCaughrean

Illustrated by Alex Wilson
and David Pavon

Cats don't like water, so you'd think they would have been first aboard. When the world was being swallowed up by water, and there stood this huge wooden ship, gangplank down and Noah beckoning the animals aboard, you'd expect the cats to be already curled up in the warmest corner of the ark.

But no. Because when the flood came, there were no cats. It happened in the Pre-Cat Age. Hard to imagine, but there you are.

Noah did not pick or choose his passengers. He had been told to take two of everything. You and I might

have left behind the scorpions, millipedes, tarantulas, and asps, but Noah invited two of everybody . . .

Except rats.

Rats nibble and gnaw. They gnaw and nibble. They also breed. Between the first flash of lightning and bang of thunder, two rats squeezed under the door, uninvited. Before the treetops were underwater, two dozen rats were scampering and scuttling, nibbling and gnawing. They ate the food meant for other animals. They left their droppings in everyone's bed. But worst of all, they gnawed and nibbled the ark itself.

"What can I do?" Noah asked the lion. Lion sneezed once and sneezed again. Perhaps it was the horses' hay tickling his nose, pollen from the bees, or dust from the donkeys. Or perhaps it was lion magic.

From out of his nose fell two balls of fluff. The fluff turned over in mid-air and landed on four paws: the world's first cats. They sprang from den to pen, from hump to rump, from table to stable, from shoulder to shelf. They hunted down the rats, and either ate them or chased them over the side. (Rats swim rather well.) The noise of scratching and scraping was gone. The cats had bounced and pounced every rat out of the ark.

Except one.

One had gnawed its way right into the wall of the ark, chewing out a hole to hide in. But rats nibble and gnaw; they gnaw and nibble; they cannot help themselves. The rat in the wall kept on gnawing.

While the floodwaters still lay deep over the mountain peaks, and the ark gently spun in the wind, Rat gnawed right through the wood.

The water outside came inside. Rat abandoned ship. The ark was leaking! Very soon, Noah, his animals, his wife, and children would sink back down to the washy wastes of an underwater world. Up came the water: up to Noah's knees, up to the eagles' beaks,

up to the ostriches' ears. Up came the water . . .

And up hopped Frog—"Ribbit ribbit"—to land in
Noah's hand. Frog took one great breath that blew
her up into a ball and, seeing her idea, Noah plugged
her into the hole. Still, droplets trickled in. Frog
spread her four tiny feet, stretched them so wide that
not one drop more could creep by her . . . and the ark
was saved.

"*Amphibious!*" cried the other animals in admiration. "Frog is absolutely and completely *amphibious!*"

And so she was. Before the flood, she had lived in bushes and trees, afraid of water, terrified of drowning. Now she held her breath, day after day, though she was seasick, sweating with fear, and her bulging eyes gazed out on dead cities, shark and squid, and a million drowned things.

When at last the ark ran aground, when the doors were opened, when the sunlight let in and the animals let out, Noah gently pulled Frog out of the hole in the hull and away she hopped. The cats thought about pouncing . . . but seeing her strange new greenness and her icky-sticky skin, they went back to hunting mice.

Noah would like to have rewarded her, but Frog had reward enough. All her tadpoles grew up green, with sticky-icky skin and feet as wide as paddles, as happy in water as they were on land.

Their proud parents thought them absolutely and completely *amphibious*.

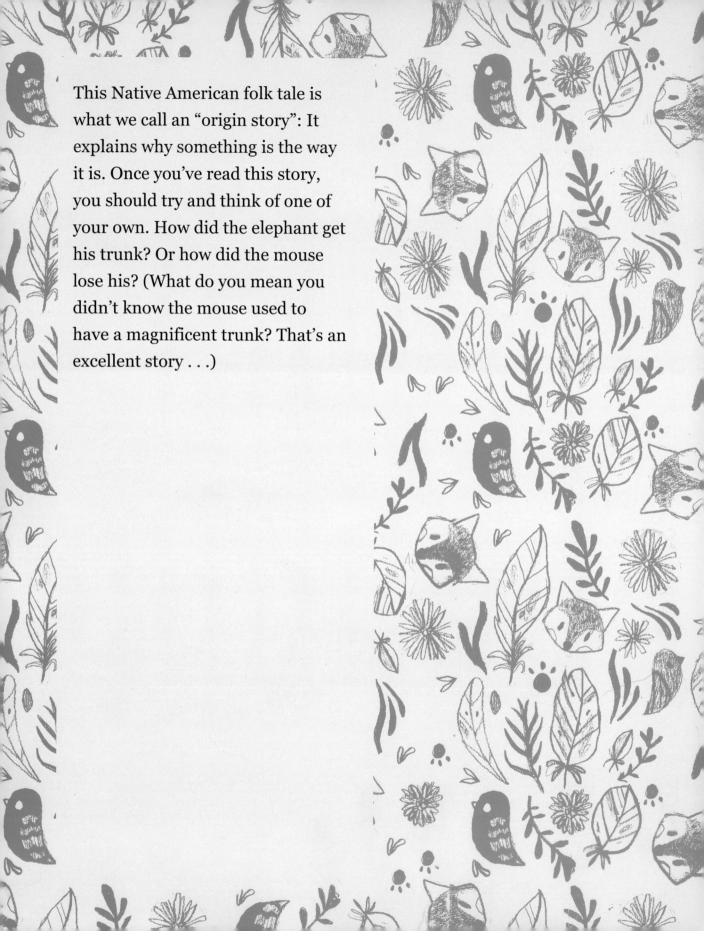

This Native American folk tale is what we call an "origin story": It explains why something is the way it is. Once you've read this story, you should try and think of one of your own. How did the elephant get his trunk? Or how did the mouse lose his? (What do you mean you didn't know the mouse used to have a magnificent trunk? That's an excellent story . . .)

How the Bear Lost His Tail

Retold by Susan Price

Illustrated by Sara Ogilvie

Bears are big, hairy, and grumpy, with short, stumpy tails.

Bears weren't always like that, though. Once, long ago, bears were different.

They were still big and hairy, but they were sweet and kind, and had long, fluffy tails. Bears were proud of their tails in those days.

How did bears get stumpy tails? Why are they so grumpy now?

Fox is to blame.

Fox was trotting around one cold day, looking for something to eat.

He saw a fisherman by a frozen lake, dangling a line through a hole in the ice.

The fisherman had caught a
lot of fish. They were lying in the
snow, tied together with string.
Fox was hungry.

Fox was sly and quick. He snuck up, grabbed the string of fish, and ran as fast as he could!

In the forest, he met Bear. Bear was hungry, too. He waved his long, fluffy tail and said, "Oh, Fox! Where did you get all those fish from?"

Fox saw that Bear's tail was even longer and fluffier than his.

Fox did not like that one bit. He did not want to share his fish, either.

So Fox said, "I caught them!"

"How?" asked Bear.

"All you have to do is break a hole in the ice on the lake," said Fox. "Then sit down and put your tail in the water."

"'It will be cold!" said Bear.

221

"Yes, but you will catch a lot of fish! Sit still, and the fish will come and nibble your tail," said Fox.

"It might hurt, but don't pull your tail out, or you will lose the fish! Your tail is so long, you will catch even more than I did!"

"Oh, thank you, Fox!" said Bear.

"Remember, don't pull your tail out too soon!" Fox said . . .

. . . and on he ran,
with his stolen fish.

Bear went down to the frozen lake. He did everything
Fox had said. He broke a hole in the ice, and put his long,
fluffy tail in the icy water.

It tingled. The water was cold! The tingling got worse as the fish began to bite. But Bear kept his tail in the water, just as Fox had said to do.

The water in the lake was so cold, the hole behind Bear began to freeze over again.

But Bear did not see.

Bear had to grit his teeth. The more it tingled, the more fish he thought he was catching.

Ouch!

But soon it was too much for Bear.

I *don't care if I lose my fish. This hurts too much!* he thought.

He tried to pull his tail out of the water.

But his tail had frozen! It snapped off like an icicle, leaving nothing but a stump. He did not even have any fish.

From that day to this, all bears have short, stumpy tails.

They are grumpy because they think everyone is laughing at them.

And Fox? Fox is still as quick and sly and clever as ever.

Bear, on the other hand, has learned that he shouldn't believe everything he is told.

Stories aren't only told through words. Many years ago, the great Russian composer, Sergei Prokofiev, created this story with music. It wasn't a musical, or an opera, simply a story told out loud—with music woven through it. It was a new kind of storytelling—musical storytelling, with different instruments, and different tunes, representing all the various characters.

I am a grandpa myself now, so I felt I would like to tell this story in a different way, as it had not been told before, from a grumpy old grandpa's point of view. So here it is. There's no music, I'm afraid, but there will be music in the words, I hope, and as you read it, you'll be picturing it in your head. It all happens in the Russian winter, deep in the forest, with snow all around. So, put on thick socks, a knit hat, and curl up somewhere warm before you start!

Peter and the Wolf

Retold by Michael Morpurgo

Illustrated by Joanna Carey

I may be a grandpa now, but once upon a time I was a little boy myself. It was a long time ago now, but I was, and I don't forget. I especially don't forget the wolf.

I lived alone with my grandpa on the edge of a deep, dark forest. "Walk off on your own into that forest, Peter," he would tell me, "and you'll get yourself lost, or, worse still, eaten by wolves. It's a great wilderness. No one lives there. It goes on forever and ever. Out there it is the wolves that do the hunting. And do you know what wolves like to eat best? Us! You! Me! But most especially, little bony boys like you. So never open the gate, Peter, do you hear me? Don't you ever go out alone into that forest. Men like me, we are hunters, we have rifles. But even we never go out alone into the forest."

He warned me often, too often. Every time he did, it only made me long to open the gate and go out into that deep, dark forest—on my own.

232

I'm not afraid, I told myself.
*I've climbed the big oak tree by the wall
and looked out over into the forest. There's
just lots of trees, and the meadow and the
pond,* I thought, *and birds, a rabbit maybe,
or a deer or two.*

233

But I've never seen a wolf. And what do I care about wolves anyway? I've seen lots of dogs in town, big ones, too, and some of them look like wolves. I just clap my hands at them, shout at them, and they run off. What's a wolf to me? I'm not afraid of wolves.

I was the kind of boy who always thought I knew best. What did my silly old grandpa know about anything?

It was one of those days—maybe once a week or so—when Grandpa went off hunting in the forest with his friends. He'd be gone all day. Every time, I would beg him to take me with him. But he never did. "When you're older," he said. Why was it that everything I wanted to do had to wait till I was older? "And besides," he went on, "it'll be too cold out there anyway. You stay here in the warmth."

It was true, it was cold—bitter cold. There was deep snow on the ground. Everything was frozen, but I still wanted to go.

The last thing he said to me was the same as it always was: "Now remember, Peter, when I'm gone, don't you dare open the gate. And don't go out into the forest, not even into the meadow, not even down to the pond. Like I told you, there are wolves out there and they eat boys, gobble them up, and chew their bones.

"Stay inside where it's warm and do your schoolwork like a good boy." And off he went, with his rifle over his shoulder.

I hated being left behind, hated doing my schoolwork. What I liked to do best of all was to climb my oak tree by the wall, sit up there in the branches with the birds, and look out over the meadow, over the pond on the edge of the forest. There were always ducks there, and I especially liked watching the ducks.

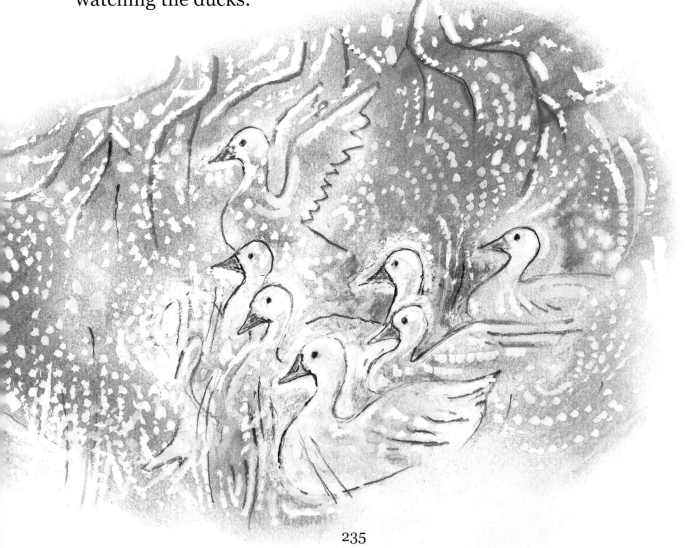

So that morning, that's what I did. There I was, sitting high in the branches of my tree. With me up there was Grandpa's ginger cat, who never stopped purring, and my little bird, a cackling laughing jay. Given half a chance, of course, the cat would eat the bird, and the bird knew it. One kept a wary eye on the other all the time.

Time and again, I told the cat, "You can eat any bird you like, but not that one." And time and again, I told the bird, "Don't get too close to the cat."

And he'd look at me. "Do you think I'm stupid?" his eyes would ask me. They were like brother and sister to me, both of them my best friends.

I had another best friend, too, though. A duck. My duck. Other ducks came and went on the pond, but the only one who was always there was my duck. That was because she had a drooping wing, a wounded wing, and could not fly. So mostly she was left alone on the pond. She was there this morning. She was always hungry.

She quacked loudly at me from the frozen pond as soon as she saw me. I knew what she wanted. Grandpa would sometimes take me with him, out of the gate and down to the pond to feed her.
So, whenever she saw
me, she thought I
had food for her.

237

"I don't have any bread. I can't feed you today," I called down from high in the tree. "I can't come down to the pond. I'm not allowed out on my own."

But she went on quacking and quacking, swimming around and around excitedly in the middle of the pond, in the little circle of water she'd managed to keep clear of ice. I could see she was starving. I had to feed her, and to do that, I would have to open the gate and go out into the meadow.

I remembered Grandpa's warnings. I knew that beyond the meadow and beyond the pond was the deep, dark forest, where the wolves lived, wolves that ate little boys and chewed their bones.

But that duck was my best friend—along with the bird and the cat. And anyway, I wasn't afraid, was I?

Quickly, I climbed down the tree and ran inside the house to fetch some bread from the kitchen.

Back outside, I opened the gate and walked out into the wide, white meadow, down toward the pond, the snow crunching under my boots.

The duck quacked loudly at me as I approached, sliding across the ice toward me. I crouched down at the edge of the pond to offer her the bread. She took it from my hand and swallowed it down, everything I gave her.

The bird flew down, cackling for some bread, too. The cat was soon there, too, eyeing the bird. "No," I told the cat firmly—I could see well enough what she had in mind. "Have some bread instead," I said. So I threw some bread crusts far out onto the snow for the cat and dropped a few breadcrumbs at my feet for the bird—which did not please the duck, of course. *But fair is fair,* I thought.

All of a sudden, a shiver
went right through me,
and I knew it wasn't the
cold. The hair stood up on
the back of my neck. The
bird screeched and flew up
into the branches of the tree.
The cat was skittering off
through the snow, yowling.
Then still yowling, she was
scrambling, scratching up the
trunk of the tree. And all the
while, the duck was quacking
loudly from the middle of the
pond. But she wasn't quacking
at me.

Something was moving at the edge of the forest. A wolf! A great, gray wolf was staring straight at me! His eyes yellow, his tongue red, his teeth sharp. I ran for it, stumbling through the snow. I could feel him coming after me—closer, closer.

I could hear the duck quacking angrily from the pond.
I reached the gate, bolted it fast behind me, and looked
out. It was the duck that had saved me. The wolf was
prowling around the pond, his eyes on the duck. This wolf
preferred duck to boy, thank goodness!

He was licking his lips. He was testing the ice with his
paw, and all the while the duck was quacking wildly at
him from her circle of water in the middle of the pond,
trying to flap her wings, trying to take off.

"Stay where you are!"
I cried. "Stay where you are!"
If only she had listened!
In her panic, she kept trying
and trying to lift off and fly.
But she couldn't fly. I knew
she couldn't. She knew she
couldn't. She got as far as
the bank and crash-landed
in the snow.

The wolf was bounding after her in an instant, racing around the lake. The duck was on her feet and half running, half flying, stumbling and tumbling, the wolf coming closer and closer all the time. Then he was on her. He had her. He swallowed her—whole.

One gulp and my duck was gone. He sat there now in the snow, staring at me, licking his lips. He was still hungry. Then, looking up, he caught sight of the cat and the bird high up in the tree, and came padding across the snow toward them.

He walked around and around the tree, his yellow eyes fixed on them, his red tongue hanging down, his teeth sharp, his tail waving high. He had eaten one of my best friends. Now he wanted the other two. As I watched, I felt the sadness inside me turning to anger, then anger growing into sudden courage.

It must have been his waving tail that gave me the idea—and his tail was, after all, the farthest away from those sharp teeth. All I needed for my plan to work was a rope—a long rope, a strong rope. I could tie a lasso in it and lower it down, wait for just the right moment.

Then pull! Yes, it could work! I'd make it work!

There was a rope hanging in Grandpa's shed. I would do it! I would do it! I'd catch that wolf!

I knew what to do. I raced across the yard to Grandpa's shed. Then, as quick as I could, I ran back over to the tree with the rope, crawling along the branch and out over the wall.

The wolf was prowling around the tree, snarling up at us. The bird flew down to be near me. He wanted to help. "Fly down," I told him, "circle around his head,

246

cackle at him, as bothersome as you can. Confuse him, make him mad." And down he flew.

I turned to the cat. "And you, hiss and yowl horribly at him, swipe your claws at him, make him madder still."

Never had the cat hissed and yowled more horribly, never had the bird's cackle been more bothersome.

As he flew around the wolf's head, the wolf was snapping and snarling, this way and that, in his fury and frustration.

And all the while,
I was making one
end of the rope into
a lasso and tying the
other end around the
branch beside me.

Then I lowered the lasso, slowly, slowly, to
the ground, and waited, waited, for the moment
when the wolf would put his paw down in
exactly the right place, inside the lasso, that

lay close to him on the ground, a trap
waiting just for him.

It took a while, a long, long while,
and I was beginning to wonder
whether I would ever catch him,
whether he would ever put his paw
in the right place. (The wrong place
for him, of course!) But then he did,
and I had him.

I jerked hard on the rope, and
pulled and pulled and pulled,
hauling him up by his foot until he
hung there, upside down in the air,
still snarling, still snapping. Was
that wolf heavy! Was he angry!
Was I huffing and puffing and
pulling with all my might!

And was I happy
to see him dangling
there at last, helpless!
We had done it! We
caught him, the bird,
the cat, and me.

That was when Grandpa and the hunters came out of the
forest, tracking the wolf's footprints. They had shot nothing.
  We had caught a wolf, alive, and it was the biggest,
angriest, snarliest wolf they had ever seen. They wanted
to shoot him there and then.

251

"No!" I cried. "He is our wolf. We have caught him, not you. So we say what happens to him. We say, let's take him to the zoo."

You should have seen us all as we made our way into town that afternoon, Grandpa and me riding in the cart, with the wolf in the back, tied up in a net, still snarling and growling. Behind came the hunters, blowing their horns, who were joined in time by drummers drumming and pipers piping. In the streets, the people clapped and cheered, and I was the hero of the hour! What a triumphant cavalcade it was! Even the cat came with us, sitting on my lap and purring happily. She had never in her life left the house before, except to catch mice and rats and birds. And the bird flew over her head, not too close, cackling and laughing.

What fun! What joy!

But suddenly, in spite of all this, I felt sad. My duck, my dearest and best of friends, was not with us. I would never hear her quacking again. Then, even as I was thinking this, I heard her. She *was* still quacking. Was it from inside the wolf maybe? No, it was inside my head. She was alive. For me, she would always be alive. I would never forget her.

"You're a very naughty boy, Peter, going out through the gate like that, when I told you not to," said Grandpa, grumpily. Then, with a smile, and a twinkle in his eye, he went on. "But you're the best and bravest grandson a grandfather ever had, that's for sure."

Acknowledgments

The following stories were commissioned for *TreeTops Greatest Stories*, *Myths and Legends*, and *Oxford Reading Tree Traditional Tales* collections and are reprinted by permission of the Author unless otherwise stated:

Authors

Brer Rabbit and the Well and *Anansi and the Antelope Baby* © Tony Bradman 2016

The Wolf in Sheep's Clothing © Pie Corbett 2010

Puss in Boots © Pippa Goodhart 2016

The Tortoise and the Baboon and *The Hungry Hyena* © Timothy Knapman 2010

When a Cat Ruled the World and *The King of Cats* © Elizabeth Laird 2010

The Magic Cow © Claire Llewellyn 2016

The Ugly Duckling, Let Me Go, and *All Aboard* © Geraldine McCaughrean 2016

Peter and the Wolf © Michael Morpurgo 2016

The Dog and His Reflection, The Farmer and the Eagle, and *The Fox and the Crow*
    © Joanna Nadin 2016

How the Bear Lost His Tail © Susan Price 2011

Illustrators

Peter and the Wolf © Joanna Carey 2016

The Wolf in Sheep's Clothing © Ester Garcia Cortes 2010

The Magic Cow © Anaïs Goldemberg 2016

Brer Rabbit and the Well and *Anansi and the Antelope Baby* © Steve Horrocks 2016

How the Bear Lost His Tail © Sara Ogilvie 2011

Puss in Boots © Thomas Radcliffe 2016

The King of Cats © Yannick Robert 2016

The Tortoise and the Baboon and *The Hungry Hyena* © Linda Selby 2010

When a Cat Ruled the World © Meilo So 2010

The Dog and His Reflection, The Farmer and the Eagle, and *The Fox and the Crow*
    © Irina Troitskaya 2016

The Ugly Duckling, Let Me Go, and *All Aboard* © Alex Wilson and David Pavon
    2016

Additional artwork and title typography © Nathan Collins